WARNING

This book contains sexually explicit scenes and adult language. It may be considered offensive to some readers. This book is for sale to adults ONLY.

* * * * * * * * * * * * * * * *

Please store your files wisely where they cannot be accessed by underage readers.

ISBN-13: 978-1987863604
ISBN-10: 1987863607

Other Books by Darla Dunbar:

<u>The Romeo Alpha BBW Paranormal Shifter Romance Series</u>

Amanda Walker thinks that she has a normal and boring life. That is until after her 24th birthday. Everything changes when she meets the man who says he was supposed to be her husband. Denying everything the man says, she fights him every step of the way. But after he kidnaps her, Amanda discovers that there are some things about her family that her parents kept a secret all these years. Among the history of the family she learns secrets she thought only happened in story books. Can Amanda tell the difference between truth and lies or is she this mysterious woman that holds the key to a legacy?

<u>Romeo Alpha Blood Lines Romance Series</u>

Twenty-four years have passed in relative peace for Amanda and Romeo. They've raised five children into adulthood and are thoroughly enjoying their lives as the Alpha King and Queen of the werewolves. At twenty-four, Sarina is just stepping into her powers and will be ripe for mating when her birthday comes in two weeks. What no one knows is the danger that lurks just outside their tight knit community. Romeo has made peace with the other clans and has enjoyed that peace, but it will all come crashing down around him when his oldest daughter comes of age to take a mate.

The Alpha Feud BBW Paranormal Shifter Romance Series

Eliza's life consisted of reporting on boring, crowd-pleasing events, like their country livestock fair. With the arrival of two handsome brothers, the lives of Eliza and her best friend, Melissa, are shaken to the core. For Eliza, the arrival of this new man becomes a test of her relationship with her current boyfriend, who she's been happily living with for over six years. Does Hayden, a complete stranger, really wield the power to make Eliza reconsider her relationship with Andrew?

The Alpha Packed BBW Paranormal Shifter Romance Series

Darlene has led a quiet life since suffering through a terrible break-up. She wants nothing more than to spend her time in front of the TV, away from any sort of trouble. But all that goes down the drain when handsome, rugged and rough Idris comes into her life. He is a werewolf on the lookout for his missing pack leader. Darlene quickly finds herself pulled towards this mysterious man and at the same time finds herself falling deeper and deeper into the world of the supernatural.

The Daemon Paranormal Romance Chronicles

The daemon infighting can only be stopped when a strong leader emerges to calm the different factions. Juno appears to be at the heart of the conflict. Things become complicated when Phoebe and Supay try to negotiate with the siren, Juno. The love triangle among Phoebe, Supay and Apollo become tense when Juno's meddling threatens to destroy any romance that develops.

<u>The Mind Talker Paranormal Romance Series</u>

Ananda finds herself on the run and she's not alone. With help from Jared, a stranger that she just met, the two evade capture by an organization that is intent on hunting her kind. Ananda and Jared are able to read minds. When an unfortunate incident happened involving a disturbed individual that resulted in the death of his schoolmates, the secret organization decided to take action.

Get the latest update on new releases from the author at:

https://darladunbar.com/newsletter/

This book is Part Three of "<u>The Leather Satchel Paranormal Romance Series</u>"

Book 1 - Valtina's Redemption

Valtina is stuck in Middle World, unable to pass on to The Afterlife. In order to redeem herself from past deeds done, she must help bring romance back into the world and stop The Dark Side from destroying love in its entirety. Following orders issued by Ladaya and armed with a leather satchel filled with the appropriate tools and weapons, Valtina must bring romance back into the lives of Samantha and Joshua, thereby saving their marriage.

Book 2 - Unfaithful

Amy and Matt's relationship was never meant to be. The evil forces at work are bent on eliminating love on Earth. Couples are being mismatched in order to create chaos. It is Valtina's mission the help Amy find her soul mate and repair the damage that is being caused by the dark forces.

Book 3 - Evil Lust

Henry and Claire are meant to be together. But a succubus has taken over Henry's actions. Under her spell, Henry has succumbed to lusting after Charlotte, the human form that the succubus has assumed. If Claire were to find out, then their marriage will be ruined beyond repair. It is up to Valtina to break the succubus' spell and clear Henry's memory of any guilt that would haunt his love for Claire forever.

Book 4 - Salvaged Soul Mates

The Dark Side is winning. A Mystic has organized the evil monsters to steal every soul on Earth and leave it loveless. It is up to Valtina to do her part to save the human race. Sent by Ladaya back to Earth, Valtina's job is to unite a mismatched couple with their true soul-mates. Sebastian and Claudia were not meant to be married to each other. But a trickster was involved in encouraging the mismatch. Searching through her leather satchel, Valtina found the tools needed to do the job.

Book 5 - Fury of Lust

Valtina's missions are becoming more dangerous and will need the protection of a warrior and emere while out on duty. This time she needs to rid Rachel of a fury and free Sean of his demons. Rachel and Sean are meant to be true lovers but they have been prevented from meeting each other. Valtina must use the arsenal in her leather satchel to ensure that true love follows its course when Rachel and Sean finally meet.

Book 6 - True Lovers

Middle World has been invaded by the wraiths. While the Generals battle the monsters to protect Middle World, Valtina must continue her missions to save love on Earth. The evil forces have brain-washed Penelope and Davis into thinking that their attraction for each other is wrong. Valtina's mission is to clear the way for the couple to see that they were meant for each other and to let true love runs its fateful course.

The Leather Satchel Paranormal Romance Series

Evil Lust

Book Three

By Darla Dunbar

Table of Contents

Chapter One

VALTINA WAITED patiently for Ladaya to return with her next assignment. She didn't know how much time had passed since she last saw her mentor. Time ran differently in Middle World, much more slowly than on Earth or in The Afterlife. Valtina had stopped trying to keep up with it several lifetimes ago, but Ladaya's absence seemed long, even by Middle World standards.

As she waited, Valtina wondered where Ladaya would send her next. She was determined to earn her way into The Afterlife, and she was full of confidence that she would be successful. Her recent mission had been challenging but rewarding… Amy and Kyle were meant to be together. Matt was a lost cause and Valtina was able to finesse the situation for the best outcome. In just two days, she was able to create a long-lasting relationship that should have happened a lot sooner. Valtina was certain she could handle any assignment Ladaya gave her.

The last assignment was actually enjoyable. In fact, Valtina would probably have accepted the mission even if Ladaya hadn't offered The Afterlife as a reward. In each of her lives, Valtina had been a passionate, sexual person. She'd never enjoyed sex just for the sake of sex. In each life she'd found her soul-mate, the one person whose spirit understood hers. And in each life, she and her soul-mate had enjoyed passionate, adventurous sex.

"I guess I am uniquely qualified for this job," Valtina thought out loud.

"You certainly are," said a familiar voice behind her. Valtina turned and found Ladaya approaching. She looked tired... and a little worried.

"Are you alright?" Valtina asked.

"It's been a long three days." Ladaya sighed. "We're losing ground. We've tapped every resource we have, but evil is still winning. Their numbers are multiplying as ours dwindle. There's still hope, of course, I just never thought it would get this far." Ladaya smiled sadly.

"What can I do, Ladaya?" Valtina asked determinedly.

"We're fighting many dark forces," Ladaya explained, "forces that for centuries were happy to fight amongst themselves. Humans have always been affected by them, but never to such a large scale. But a few decades ago, these forces decided to unite under a common goal. Since then, their sole focus has been to end existence as we know it. And, as you know, the only way to do that is to rid the world of love. If the last drop of love dies, every living organism will follow... the barren earth will be left to every foul creature that's ever been created. I'm sorry if this sounds repetitive, Valtina, but you MUST understand the importance of your missions."

"I understand, Ladaya. Just tell me where to go next."

"This case is much different than your last mission," Ladaya began. "Claire and Henry are married, and they're meant to be. But there are forces working against them… powerful forces. In fact, Valtina, I'm about to put you up against, essentially, your evil twin."

"My evil twin? I'm afraid I'm going to need you to explain that," Valtina said, taken aback.

"Think, Valtina. Your strength, your love, your goodness, they're all rooted in your sexuality. What's the evil counterpart to that?"

Valtina thought for a moment, and then gasped. "You can't be serious," she said firmly. "They don't exist. Not anymore."

"That's what we thought, but we were wrong. I think they've been waiting… the other creatures have set everything up just right, and now they've come out of hiding and they're moving in for the final play."

"So… you're sending me after…"

"Yes. A succubus," Ladaya interrupted. "I'm not sure of her true name, but Henry knows her as Charlotte. It's important that we move quickly. Henry has only been under her spell for a few days. Claire and Henry have a nine-month-old baby, so Claire is distracted and hasn't noticed any change in her husband. If we can keep her from finding out, we can save their marriage. We could wipe her memory, but we can't erase the scars left by that deep of a betrayal. If she learns of Henry's infidelity, their love will die."

"We won't let evil win, Ladaya. I'll do my best work." Valtina took her leader by the hand and met her eyes. "My absolute best work. I promise."

"You must, Valtina." She sighed, squeezing her hand. "Once you've broken the spell Charlotte has on Henry, wipe his memory of her. He isn't cheating on purpose… she has total control. This isn't something he should suffer for."

"But how do I break the spell?" Valtina asked.

"Follow your instincts," Ladaya smiled. "This is one area in which they've always served you well. Now, you'd probably be able to spot the succubus anyway, but your new powers will allow you to see her true form. You'll see the true form of other creatures as well. Do NOT react when you see them. Some monsters can see spirits, so you don't want to draw attention to yourself. If you're ever in true danger I'll sense it, and I'll send help immediately."

Valtina wasn't scared. As a matter of fact, this was the most exhilarated she'd felt since she entered Middle World. Once again, she had a purpose, a reason for being. "What do you want me to do with the succubus after I've broken her spell?" she asked fiercely.

"Nothing," Ladaya responded firmly. "You are to focus on your mission, and your mission alone. We have others in our ranks who are equipped to fight monsters. But the connection between her and Henry must be broken first, or anything we do to her will happen to him too."

"I'll do it as quickly as possible," Valtina promised. "I'll see you soon." She smiled at Ladaya as the fog surrounded her, transporting her to Henry and Claire's bedroom.

Chapter Two

It took a moment for Valtina's eyes to adjust to the darkness of the room. Before she could see, she sensed that Claire and Henry were both awake, and both pretending not to be. She'd practiced her new abilities while waiting for this assignment… she entered Claire's mind first. As Valtina had expected, the woman's mind was mostly occupied with thoughts of her son. "Is he sleeping? Is he breathing? Maybe tomorrow he'll take his first steps!" It wasn't until Valtina reached the back of Claire's mind that she found thoughts of Henry. "I wonder if he's having a hard time at work. I wonder if he's jealous of the baby… the magazines said that could happen. Oh! The baby! Maybe he'll take his first steps tomorrow!"

Valtina left Claire's mind. It wasn't hard to spot the problem in there! Claire had stopped thinking about her husband almost completely. It was no wonder she hadn't noticed any changes in her husband. That was convenient, for the time being, but Valtina knew she would have to work hard to direct Claire's thoughts to Henry.

Valtina entered Henry's mind, curious about what she would find. The man's thoughts were split equally between guilt and desire. It was obvious to Valtina that Henry loved his wife. And he didn't love Charlotte. But for some reason he couldn't stay away from her. He didn't WANT her, but he NEEDED her. Valtina felt Henry's pain and confusion, and it was too much to bear. She left his mind quickly, and studied the couple while she came up with a plan. In Henry's mind, she'd learned that he had a secret lingerie fetish. Charlotte had obviously read his mind too. Valtina had watched memories of the succubus seducing him in sexy, slutty outfits. That was something she could work with. She held her leather satchel close, and rested the minds of her new charges. Tomorrow would be a busy day, and they needed their rest.

The next morning, Valtina waited in the bedroom until Henry emerged and hastily left for work. Once he was gone, Valtina browsed through the contents of her leather satchel and pulled out a pair of sheer, black nylon stockings with back seams and a sexy black garter belt. She laid them neatly on the bed, and then set off to find Claire and the baby.

She found them in the living room, spread out on the carpet and laughing at a cartoon on television. Or rather, the baby was laughing at the cartoon, while Claire laughed at the baby. "Oh James, you're such a silly boy." Claire laughed. Valtina took the opportunity to jog Claire's memory.

Claire watched her son, so carefree, so happy. When he laughed, her heart filled with a joy she'd never known. It struck her, suddenly, how very much her son reminded her of his father. They had the same eyes, the same smile, even the same laugh. She watched the baby make faces at the characters on the screen, and was filled with gratitude and love for her husband for giving her their family.

Claire thought of the night James was conceived. She and Henry had only been married for six months, and they'd already been trying to get pregnant for three. That night, in the hot, steamy shower, Claire had known they'd made a baby. She couldn't explain it, but she'd been certain. And she'd been right. Henry had been the perfect husband throughout her pregnancy, always there but never hovering. Come to think of it, Henry had always been a great husband. Suddenly, Claire missed her husband terribly. She couldn't remember the last time they'd made love and now that was all she wanted to do.

"I wonder if Daddy can cut out of work early today," she said out loud to the baby as she called Henry's cell phone. After four rings, his voicemail picked up. Claire hung up without leaving a message. She got James down for a nap, and then walked into her bedroom and discovered the stockings and garter belt. A rush of exhilaration ran through her. "I guess Henry's missing me too," Valtina heard her think. Satisfied that Claire's attention was focused in the right place, Valtina left to find Henry.

Valtina's powers guided her to a coffee shop on the opposite side of town. She entered, and found Henry sitting with what would have been a beautiful woman, if not for the forked tongue and tail. Valtina entered Henry's mind… she wasn't surprised to find that no thoughts of Claire remained in his head. Instead, Henry was completely fixated on Charlotte. "She's so beautiful. Why is she interested in me? I'd give everything I have to be with her." After listening in on Henry, Valtina knew she had to work quickly. Her powers weren't as strong as the succubus', but Valtina had love on her side. "There's something not quite right about Charlotte." Valtina concentrated on the thought.

Henry shifted uncomfortably in his seat and met Charlotte's eyes. "There's something wrong with her," he thought. "I can't put my finger on what… but something's definitely not right." Valtina shifted her concentration to Claire. "She's not Claire," Henry realized. "What am I doing here? I LOVE Claire!"

Valtina listened to Henry's thoughts, but her concentration was interrupted by a shrill, high-pitched wail. Charlotte had realized that her connection to Henry had been broken, and she was angry. Valtina watched the succubus' eyes turn red and remembered Ladaya's promise… if she was ever in danger, help would be sent. Surprisingly, Valtina was the only one who seemed to notice Charlotte's transformation… she wondered what the other people in the coffee shop were seeing.

"The humans think they're watching a lover's quarrel," a voice said over Valtina's shoulder. Startled, she jumped forward and turned around.

"I didn't mean to scare you." The male spirit smiled. "I'm here to deal with the aftermath of this, once you get Henry safely out of the coffee shop. I'm Demetri, by the way."

Valtina smiled at her fellow warrior. Demetri was tall and muscular, with broad shoulders, sandy blonde hair, and deep green eyes. She smoothed her raven hair before speaking.

"I'm Valtina." She smiled. "Can you help me? How am I supposed to get Henry away from her? Ladaya told me to follow my instincts, and I DID break her spell, but how do I separate them?"

"You've done your job," Demetri explained. "Henry is breaking things off with her. You can't hear it, over that god-awful siren wail, but he'll leave on his own soon enough. And then I'll stop her from following," he said simply.

Valtina was excited by Demetri. He was sexy, confident, and he knew how to kill evil. She was disappointed when Henry stood up to leave… she'd hoped for more time with Demetri, she had so many questions. She gave him one last smile before turning to follow Henry out the door.

"It was nice to meet you, Valtina," Demetri called after her. "I'm sure we'll meet again soon." Valtina smiled to herself as she followed Henry to his car.

The moment the car doors shut, Valtina entered Henry's mind again. "What have I done? What have I DONE?! What if Claire…" The thought terminated the moment Valtina erased Charlotte from Henry's mind. "What am I doing here?" Henry thought with confusion. Valtina continued her work. "Oh, that's right! I left work early to find a present for Claire. She really deserves something. She's such a fantastic mother… and sexy! She's so sexy!" Henry thought. Valtina smiled as he left the car again and walked to the adult store across the street from the coffee shop. Confident that Henry was in good shape, Valtina left to provide Claire with some inspiration.

Chapter Three

Valtina was shocked when she returned to the house. An older woman, who Valtina immediately knew was Claire's favorite aunt, was leaving with James.

"Thank you so much, Aunt Alice," Claire smiled nervously.

"Thank you! I've been begging for a slumber party with this little man for months! Now don't you worry! James and I will be just fine. And if it gets too hard for you just call and I'll bring him right home."

"I'm going to try to make it." Claire laughed. "But don't be surprised if you get a 2 a.m. phone call." Valtina felt Claire's twinge of pain as Alice's car disappeared down the street. "No need for that." Valtina thought. The anxiety instantly left Claire. "Hmm… what should I wear with the stockings and garter?" she thought to herself. Claire didn't have any lingerie, so she put on her husband's surprise then pulled one of her go-to maxi dresses over her head. "This will just have to do," she sighed. As she opened the bedroom door she heard the garage door open. "What's Henry doing home so early?" she thought to herself. "What does it matter? He's here! Go get him!" Another voice in her head replied. She agreed with the second voice, and rushed downstairs to greet her husband.

Henry was so happy to see his wife he didn't notice the black stockings peeking out from the bottom of her dress. "There's my beautiful wife." He smiled. He was overwhelmed with desire for his wife. He'd seen her in that exact same dress many times throughout her pregnancy and after. But he'd never until that moment noticed how the top cupped the shape of her breasts, or how the fabric moved ever so gently across her hips.

"Henry! I've missed you today! I tried to call earlier. I have a surprise," she hinted mischievously.

"I have several for you too." Henry smiled and held a large shopping bag out to his wife. Claire took the bag and quickly opened it.

"Henry!" she gasped. She'd never seen such scandalous lingerie, but instead of being embarrassed by it, she became emboldened. She held up a sheer black nylon teddy. It was incredibly short, lacy, and had holes cut out at the nipples.

"I know we'll have to wait until we get James down, but what do you say? Want to try that on for me later?" Henry teased. To his shock, Claire met his eyes, and then dropped her dress to the ground. A wide smile broke across Henry's face. "Is he already asleep?" he asked hopefully, longing to release his growing erection from the confines of his slacks.

"He's having a slumber party with Alice," Claire answered as she put on the teddy. She smiled as she modeled for her husband. "Now, where do you want me?" she asked seductively. Instead of answering, Henry pulled her close and kissed her fiercely.

He picked her up and carried her to the couch. "Here is good for now," he mumbled as he nibbled and sucked at her exposed nipples. "I'm going to make love to you all night," Henry promised. "I'm going to lick, and kiss, and enjoy every inch of your body." He moved his lips to her stomach and kissed her through the nylon. Claire arched towards him and guided his hands back to her breasts. "But first Claire, first I'm going to take you, right here. I have to have you. I have to have you," he moaned as he rubbed his stiff, throbbing cock against the cool, silky nylon.

"Take me. Give it to me now!" Claire replied urgently. She moved to position her hips under Henry's, but he had something else in mind. He lifted her again, and sat her on the arm of the couch, with her legs over the side. He gently laid her back on the cushion, placing her head significantly lower than her hips.

"I want to be able to see all of you," he explained. "You look so fucking hot in that outfit baby." He leaned over and kissed her stomach again as he took her hips in his hands. He placed one finger between her legs, and finding her dripping wet, stood and entered her in one fluid motion.

Claire gasped with pleasure as she felt Henry's cock hit her deepest place. The odd angle of their position made it difficult for Claire to match her husband's thrusts, so she squeezed him with her pussy muscles instead.

"Oh God, you feel so amazing," Henry moaned. "How do you want it baby? Do you like it like that?" He asked as he increased his speed. Claire couldn't respond. Having her hips elevated was allowing Henry to hit her G-Spot with every thrust. She felt herself climbing to an orgasm and she didn't want anything to interrupt it. Spurred on by her moans and cries, Henry continued to increase the speed and force of his thrusts. Soon, Claire was overwhelmed by the deepest, most intense orgasm she'd ever experienced. It wasn't until she regained control of her senses that she realized Henry had replaced his cock with his tongue, and was probing and lapping hungrily. The stimulation was almost more than Claire could take, but Henry wouldn't allow her to pull away. When he was finally satisfied, he reached up for the blanket on the couch and then rolled Claire down into his lap.

"Oh my God baby, if that orgasm had been any stronger it would have killed me. But why did you stop?" she asked, taking his still rigid cock in her hand. She began stroking him lightly. Henry pulled away enough to make eye contact with his wife.

"You mean… you didn't realize?" he asked incredulously. He smiled. "You came so hard you squirted," he explained, thrusting into the hand wrapped around his erection. "I had to taste it." He smiled, and then nuzzled under her ear. "I've never tasted anything so delicious," he murmured. "And it is now my personal mission to make you do that all of the time."

He nibbled her collar bone before taking a nipple into his mouth. He teased it with his tongue, sucked roughly, and then carefully bit down. Claire cried in delight… she instantly wanted Henry's cock inside of her again, but decided to treat him to a little oral first. She pulled away, rolled her husband onto his back, and straddled his stomach.

"Have I told you how sexy you look?" Henry asked. As she leaned down to kiss him, her exposed nipples grazed his chest. He reached for them, but Claire pulled away. She lay next to Henry, placing her feet near his head.

Claire was in no mood to tease her husband. Instead, she took the full length of his cock down her throat. Henry groaned and stroked Claire's nylon covered legs. Valtina noticed how much the fabric aroused Henry, and planted an idea in Claire's head for later. As Claire continued to bob up and down on her husband's cock, Henry reached over and pulled her up to lay across him.

He put a hand on each side of Claire's pussy and began firmly massaging her outer lips. The massage was just stimulating enough to leave Claire wanting more… she pulled away from his thick, dripping cock long enough to beg "Please." Henry relented, and slowly eased three fingers inside of her. It didn't take long for Claire to realize that he was matching his strokes to hers. Soon, Claire felt a second climax approaching.

With one hand she pulled the teddy over her head and let it fall around Henry's cock. She licked and teased the tip with her mouth as she wrapped the nylon around his shaft. She gripped Henry through the fabric and stroked him firmly. Henry responded by rubbing her clit with his thumb, gently at first, and then more forcefully. They came at the same time, filling each other's mouths with the juices of their love.

Valtina watched with satisfaction as the couple curled up in each other's arms. They lay like that for several minutes, silently, until at last Claire pulled away.

"I bought snacks." She smiled as she rose and sashayed to the kitchen. She'd hoped the evening would provide them with plenty of opportunities to work up an appetite and no spare time to cook. She pulled a meat, cheese, and cracker tray out of the refrigerator and returned to her husband.

"Just like the old days." Henry laughed when he saw the tray. Henry and Claire had spent the first few months of their marriage in bed. They'd only emerged from their apartment to work and to stock up on ready-to-eat snack trays at the deli on the ground floor of their building.

"I've missed the old days," Claire confessed. "I'm not saying I'm not happy now… I just miss the newness, and the excitement of it all."

Henry swallowed, then responded "I know how you feel. I feel the same way… but maybe we can start exploring new things together, get those feelings back," he suggested sweetly. "I'm proud of you by the way, for letting Alice take James. We've needed some quality time together."

"I don't know why I was so worried about it, honestly." Claire confessed. "I think we should let him go more often. Mommy and daddy need alone time," she flirted. Henry watched his wife. The sight of her, sitting and carrying on a conversation while wearing only the garter belt and one stocking was making him hard again. And since he was still completely naked, Claire noticed.

"My, my… someone can't seem to get enough," she teased. She crawled over to James and he took her into his arms.

"I'll never get enough Claire," he replied seriously. "I love you so much. I sometimes forget to tell you, and to show you. I'm going to do better, I promise."

Claire sighed. "I'm going to do better too, Henry. I'm going to pay you more attention… and act like your wife again… I'm going to remember that we're a couple… a hot, sexual couple… and not just parents."

"We are incredibly hot," Henry smiled as he leaned in to caress his wife's neck. "You are incredibly hot," he said as he removed her second stocking. "And as promised, I'm going to continue making love to you all night." He gently laid Claire on her back and parted her legs. He eased in to her and then braced Claire with one hand and rolled carefully until they were on their sides. Claire squeezed his cock lightly, making eye contact with Henry. He moved back and forth ever so slightly, embracing his wife and meeting her gaze.

"This is how we belong," Claire said with a soft moan. "Connected… together… I wish I could keep you in me always." Henry slightly increased the speed of this movement and Claire responded by squeezing him tighter. Valtina watched them continue that way for over an hour. They lay connected, moving softly and slowly, all the while expressing their feelings for each other.

A single tear fell down Valtina's cheek. What she was witnessing reminded her so much of each of her lives. How she used to love making slow, sensual, passionate love to her soul-mates. In fact, she had played out almost this exact scene with each of them. She wondered for a moment if she would meet them again in The Afterlife, or if she would find unexpected, new love there.

Her biggest fear was that she'd be alone in The Afterlife, just as she was in Middle World. Valtina was brought back to the present by the increased volume of Henry and Claire's cries. Valtina knew that once again, they'd climaxed together. She entered each of their minds again, and found only contented, peaceful happiness. As Henry and Claire fell asleep in each other's arms, Valtina was once again surrounded by the white fog and transported back to Middle World.

Chapter Four

Valtina expected a warm, congratulatory welcome from Ladaya. After all, she'd just successfully completed her third assignment. She'd defeated a succubus and rekindled a true love match, all in less time than her first, easier assignment. But there was no joy or pride in Ladaya's face when she arrived for Valtina's report. She looked more frustrated and disheveled than she had the previous day.

"You did very well Valtina," Ladaya sighed with exhaustion.

"Then why do you look so upset?" Valtina responded. "Did I do something wrong? She felt me, didn't she? When I inspired Claire to run and greet Henry? She knew I was in her head." She sighed in defeat.

"No, Valtina. You've done nothing to upset me, and Claire never suspected that thought wasn't hers. My mind is in other places right now, but be assured that you've made me incredibly proud. No one has been able to break a succubus's spell so quickly, and completely, and you are finishing your assignments much faster than the others." Ladaya smiled for a moment before furrowing her brow once more. "That's the problem, you see. The other side is working so much faster than we are. For every problem we resolve, they create a dozen more… literally. The monsters are breeding like mad…"

"How badly are we outnumbered, Ladaya?" Valtina asked nervously.

"I don't even know how many of them there are… but I'd say 20 to 1 is a conservative estimate," Ladaya admitted. Valtina took a moment to let the news sink in. When Ladaya had first approached her, she'd thought she'd get to move on to The Afterlife after that first mission. It was becoming more and more apparent that her reward was as far away as it had ever been. If she moved on to The Afterlife, she wouldn't be able to return to Earth… she'd be like Ladaya, only able to view mankind from a distance. And Ladaya had made it clear how much she was needed on Earth.

Valtina considered the situation for a long time, while Ladaya stood silently, allowing her to think. Valtina longed for peace, and felt she deserved it after all of the progress she'd made in Middle World. But didn't everyone else deserve peace too? Valtina suddenly realized that if The Afterlife was more important to her than the survival of the Earth, she didn't deserve it. With a deep breath, she fully accepted her fate and responsibility.

"Ladaya, I will fight until the end," she vowed. "I will do everything in my power to help true love thrive. And I won't quit until the Earth has been rid of evil for good."

Tears welled in Ladaya's eyes. "Valtina, you don't know how much I wish I could reward you now. If there's anything I can do for you, please just ask."

"You could answer a question for me," Valtina hesitated, remembering the tear she shed while watching Henry and Claire make love.

"What would you like to know?"

"Once this is over, and I get to move on, will I meet any of my soul-mates in The Afterlife? Does love… romantic love… exist there?"

"Valtina! I'd have thought you would have figured this out by now!" Ladaya exclaimed.

"Figured what out?"

"Think Valtina. You've lived several different lives, with several different names," Ladaya prompted slowly.

"Yes…"

"But in each life you were essentially the same person. You improved with each life, of course, but your strengths, your weaknesses, the structure of who you are was always the same." Ladaya paused for a moment, waiting for Valtina to understand. When she didn't, Ladaya continued. "And in each life you found your soul-mate… the one person whose foundation complemented yours."

Realization spread across Valtina's face. "He was always the same person," she said out loud.

"Yes," Ladaya smiled. "He was always the same person. Which makes it all the more phenomenal that you found each other in every life. You were matched together in The Before, and you will be reunited in The Afterlife."

"So he's there?" Valtina asked hopefully.

"Not yet. Like you, he's working towards redemption."

"He's here? In Middle World? If he's working against the evil forces too, couldn't we work together?"

"That's not how it works, Valtina. Just as you didn't recognize him from life to life, you won't recognize him here. And we have more important matters at hand. But you can rest assured, when you both reach The Afterlife and possess your true forms, you'll be united in bliss like nothing you experienced in any of your lifetimes."

Valtina was overwhelmed with hope and determination. With the promise of an eternity with her true love, she was eager to begin her next assignment and move closer to her reward.

"Where am I going next, Ladaya? Another succubus? A different kind of monster?"

"No," Ladaya answered gravely, "not this time. Unfortunately evil doesn't reside in monsters alone. There are plenty of humans working against us too, and it takes great skill and patience to rid their hearts of the evil that controls them. Do you think you're up to the task?"

"Absolutely," Valtina answered with confidence. She filled her mind with thoughts of her true love while Ladaya returned to The Afterlife to view the Earth and determine where Valtina was needed next.

-To be continued in Book 4-

If you enjoyed this title, I would appreciate your leaving a review of the book. Good reviews encourage an author to write as well as help books to sell. Good reviews can be just a few short sentences describing what you liked about the book without having a spoiler. If you could spend 30 seconds writing a review, I would appreciate it: you can review this title right now at your favorite retailer.

Here is a preview of the **next story** you may enjoy:

**Salvaged Soul Mates - The Leather Satchel
Romance Series, Book 4**

VALTINA SAT under a tree in Middle World,
observing the spirits around her. She'd been scanning
the faces of those who passed ever since Ladaya had
told her that her soul-mate was also stuck in Middle
World. She tried to sense his spirit, but as her mentor
had warned, she hadn't recognized him yet. Valtina
contented herself to sitting still and watching as the
others moved about. Like her, many had been enlisted
to fight in the war against evil. Middle World was
frequently filled with visitors from The Afterlife.
Generals, like Ladaya, popped in to give instructions
and updates to their soldiers. Valtina hadn't seen
anyone she recognized, though several of her friends
had already moved on.

As Valtina waited she thought about her mission.
The last one had been more difficult than the previous
one, as she'd had to break the spell of a succubus. And
Ladaya had warned her that all varieties of monsters
were fighting for the other side. She wondered what
kind of danger she would encounter next. Valtina's
thoughts were interrupted when Ladaya appeared
before her. She was frazzled, and seemed to be on the
verge of tears.

"Ladaya! What's happened?" Valtina asked in a
panic.

"I've just been observing," Ladaya sobbed, "the
mist… the black mist of evil… it's growing. I watched

it spread before my eyes. Oh Valtina, I don't know what we're going to do."

"Do you know what's making it spread so quickly?"

"We do. One of our under-covers reported in yesterday, and confirmed our worst fear. The driving force behind the other army is a creature that was believed to be a thing of legend. No one in my time, or the times of those before me, has ever encountered one. It is a thing so evil it cannot be killed. Part demon, part witch, she's rumored to be the spawn of a warlock and something very unnatural he conjured in his bedroom. Her powers are innumerable, and, I'm afraid, impossible to defeat. She's bred a wraith army; their sole purpose is to steal every soul on Earth. As you know, without a soul, one cannot feel love. If we don't stop them soon, it will all be over." Ladaya sighed.

"This creature… you don't mean a Mystic?!" Valtina asked with alarm.

"I'm afraid so." Ladaya nodded. "They call her Morgonda. We're quite certain she's the one who organized the monsters against us. Her goal is to rid the world of living creatures, and reign as Queen of the monsters.

"What can I do?" Valtina asked quickly. "How can we defeat them? Tell me how, Ladaya. Surely we need everyone focused on this right now. I can fix people's love lives once we've defeated them!"

"Valtina, I appreciate your offer. But it's important that we take advantage of each spirit's strengths. We have others who are more fitted to destroying evil, and you are too valuable in your area for us to risk you! But be aware, the wraiths can see you. Remember, their sole purpose is to steal souls… As you are nothing but a soul, you'd be an easy job for them. But, as usual, should you encounter one, help will appear."

"That's ridiculous, Ladaya," Valtina argued. "Don't the 'qualified' spirits have more important things to do than rescue me? Tell me how to take them out myself," she insisted.

Ladaya sighed. "Really, Valtina, I don't want you anywhere near them. There are rules for a reason, and you are no exception. And I believe that's one of the things you're in Middle World to work on? Following *directions*?" Ladaya reminded her sharply. Valtina sighed. It was true that in all of her lifetimes, she'd had a bit of a problem following the rules. Even really important rules she'd ignore, just for the sake of ignoring them. The Supreme Ruler in The Afterlife felt she needed some more practice in listening to authority before she moved on.

"I'm sorry, Ladaya. You're right," Valtina conceded. "What are my instructions? What's my next mission? The faster I get started, the faster I can move on to the next one, right?" She smiled.

Ladaya softened. "Well, as I told you, humans are spreading the evil almost as quickly as the monsters. Morgonda has sent these humans helpers, in the form of tricksters. They make sure the humans' plans fall into place, and that the plans of those around them fall apart.

I'm afraid they've been at work since long before we knew of The Dark Side's plans. The couple I'm sending you to next has been affected by a trickster for five years. They're a mismatched couple, you see, put together by their fathers as a part of a master business plan. The fathers sold their souls to a demon years ago, in exchange for success in their law firm. One man pressured his son to follow in his footsteps… the other did the same to his daughter. It seemed only natural to the two men that their children should marry, and keep the fortune within the two families. Claudia, the wife, fell in love with a man she met as an undergrad. Albert was smart and handsome, but seeking a teaching degree, which Claudia's father thought beneath his daughter. Sebastian, the husband, hasn't met his soul-mate yet. They were supposed to get together three years ago. So far, she hasn't encountered evil yet, and is still waiting for him.

"The trickster attached to Claudia and Sebastian's fathers put many obstacles in Albert's way, making it seem as if his relationship with Claudia was a lost cause. The trickster also made sure that Sebastian was in the right place at the right time to comfort Claudia after Albert disappeared. Then, the trickster inspired lust between the two. As soon as their fathers realized they were sleeping together, they insisted upon a wedding. The trickster was still doing his job, and inspiring lust between the couple. He's been dealt with, and now we need you to break up Sebastian and Claudia, and reunite them with their soul-mates," Ladaya finished.

"Consider it done, Ladaya," Valtina promised. "I'll return soon. I pray I come back to good news."

"That makes two of us." Ladaya smiled sadly.

The white fog enveloped Valtina and transported her to Claudia and Sebastian's townhouse. Valtina arrived early on a Saturday afternoon, and found the couple in separate rooms of the house. Claudia sat in the living room, absentmindedly watching a week's worth of recorded television. Valtina entered her mind for a moment. "What in the world has come over me?" Claudia thought. "He's my husband. I MARRIED him for Christ sake. Why am I suddenly looking at him like he's my brother? What am I going to do?"

Valtina felt sorry for Claudia. She didn't realize that she'd been under the influence of a trickster. All she knew was that suddenly, she wasn't attracted to her husband anymore. Valtina could read that Claudia still loved Sebastian very much, but not in a sexual way. The woman was fighting anxiety over what she would do the next time Sebastian propositioned her. "I just can't do it," she kept thinking to herself over and over again. "But why can't I just do it?" Valtina wanted to take the anxiety from Claudia, but felt it may be best to let it work to her advantage. She left the woman in the living room and glided through the townhouse to find Sebastian.

Valtina found him sitting in his study, attempting to focus on depositions for his upcoming trial. Like his wife, he was distracted by thoughts and feelings he didn't understand. Valtina entered his mind. "It's just a phase," he was assuring himself. "All married couples go through stuff like this. It will pass. We've always had such a hot sex life. We were bound to hit a dry spell at some point." But Valtina could tell that he didn't believe his own reassurances. He was now no more attracted to Claudia than she was to him.

Valtina thought this may be her easiest job yet. With the trickster gone, the couple was sure to part on their own. She wondered why Ladaya hadn't waited until the couple had already split. It seemed all there was for her to do was to sit back and wait until the couple parted. Then she could match them with their soul-mates. Valtina returned to the living room, sat on the couch, and watched television with Claudia for the rest of the day.

Much to Valtina's surprise, the couple carried on as usual on Saturday night and Sunday. They slept curled together in bed, they got up early and attended morning mass, and they dined at the same restaurant they always visited for Sunday brunch. It wasn't until later Sunday afternoon, when Claudia received a phone call from her father that things started to change. Valtina entered her mind, hoping to hear both sides of the conversation. But instead of being able to hear Claudia's father's words, all Valtina heard was the fear and terror in Claudia's mind. "I have to get over this… I have to find a way to make it work with Sebastian… Daddy will never understand… I don't think I could take the lectures from him if I ended things. What would happen to the firm?" Valtina left Claudia's mind… she'd heard all she needed to know. She entered Sebastian's mind and heard similar thoughts about both of their fathers. Valtina realized then why she'd been sent so soon… neither member of the couple would risk their fathers' wrath without some serious inspiration.

Valtina consulted her trusty leather satchel, looking for tools to aid her in her mission. The contents of the satchel changed with every mission. This time she found a college yearbook, a flyer for an art show, and a coupon for free admittance to a local club. Valtina's powers told her that the yearbook and the coupon should be left for Claudia, while the flyer would inspire Sebastian. She spilled a large box in Claudia's closet and placed the yearbook on top of the pile. Then, Valtina placed the flyer in Sebastian's briefcase… the coupon she would hold on to for now.

As Valtina had hoped, Claudia found the yearbook when she went to put away her shoes and lay out clothes for the next day. Valtina felt a sadness wash over Claudia, who quickly hid the book beneath her robe. She poked her head into Sebastian's study on her way to the couple's library.

If you enjoyed this sample then look for **Salvaged Soul Mates - The Leather Satchel Romance Series, Book 4.**

Here is a preview of **another story** you may enjoy:

Forgotten - The Daemon Paranormal Romance Chronicles, Book 3

ROLLING OUT of bed, Phoebe looked on Supay's sleeping form. After spending several weeks with him in Puerto Rico, she decided to move back to Peru, where he lived for most of the year. Her life had taken a strange turn. Instead of working at her fortune telling shop, she was now essentially a kept woman. During the day, they worked together to stop the fighting that kept breaking out in the daemon world. The daemons were essentially a different type of human, and each daemon possessed a unique power. Phoebe could read minds, while Supay could transform into any animal. These unique abilities had given rise to the ancient mythologies of past years. In honor of their ancestors, Phoebe's daemon family had chosen to name all of their children after Greek gods and prophets.

Phoebe threw on a robe and turned on the shower. Over the last few months, she had learned that she was a daemon and that she still had a mother. Her mother, Rhea, had been raped and conceived twin girls. Her twin sister had never made it past birth, but Phoebe had been born. With her gift of mind-reading, she had been in constant pain as an infant because she could see her mother's memories of the rape. Traumatized by the rape and inability to touch her daughter, Rhea had placed Phoebe in foster care. Phoebe finally found out that she was a daemon and about the true story when Apollo came looking for help with killing the Qilin.

Stepping into the shower, Phoebe let the warm water drift along her body. The sensation was pleasant and woke her up. Today, she needed to go with Supay to meet a daemon called Juno. According to the reports, Juno was the daemon behind much of the infighting. With the death of the Qilin, a leader was supposed to appear that would bring peace. According to prophecy, it seemed like Apollo should have been that person. Since he was still brooding over beer about the loss of Phoebe and the killing of the Qilin, Supay had convinced Phoebe that they needed to take action together.

Phoebe heard the shower curtain open. Turning, she saw…

If you enjoyed this sample then look for **Forgotten - The Daemon Paranormal Romance Chronicles, Book 3**.

Here is a preview of **another story** you may enjoy:

**Rapid Pulse Bounty - Obsessed Bounty Hunter
Romance Series, Book 3 by Carla Coxwell**

JACQUI SCHNEIDER gazed at her naked reflection
in the mirror and liked what she saw. She had always
been curvaceous since her breasts started to form when
she was sixteen years old. She got that from her mom.
But unlike her mom, whose modest virtues bordered on
obsessive, Jacqui loved to flaunt her sexiness even as a
teenage girl.

But since hooking up with Uncle Max at *The
Agency*, the daily rigors of the exercise routines the old
man made her go through every day certainly have
managed to give her muscles the tone that wasn't there
before.

Her shoulders seemed broader, giving the illusion of
a smaller waistline that curved down to her hips. Her
round ass was perky as she gave it a playful smack. Her
toned arms and legs gave her body the overall
impression of a well-oiled machine. Sweating profusely
after a five mile run, her sunburned milky-white skin
had a pinkish tinge.

After her first assignment went better than expected,
Jacqui gained a certain confidence that she never felt
before. The next three captures were just as successful.
Everything was going well for her. The changes she
saw in her body were merely icing on the cake.

Every successful capture meant more money in her
pocket. It would never replace the loneliness she felt in
being alone without mom, dad, and Danny, but it was a
good start. Jacqui mulled over in her mind how to

spend some of it. Travel, perhaps? But that decision was a long way off from today.

The thought that she would never have to worry about money in the future gave her a sense of security she lost when her whole family was murdered. The easy fifty thousand dollars that she earned from four bounty works had been deposited in the bank, together with the money her dad left her.

"Not bad…" Jacqui whispered in approval over her finances as well as the reflection staring back at her.

Picking up the heap of dirty clothes from the floor and grabbing a robe along the way, Jacqui entered the bathroom of her new apartment.

Uncle Max helped her settle into her new digs. He insisted that Jacqui come down to the headquarters every day and keep up with her training. So Jacqui opted for a modest townhouse in a quiet neighborhood five miles away. It was a two bedroom affair, furnished, thus sparing her the tedious task of shopping for her own furniture. The living room and kitchen were roomy enough to keep her comfortable during the times she was home.

The only indulgence she added was a shower stall with overhead rainfall shower, a handheld shower hose and 6 body jets. Plus the whirlpool bathtub that Uncle Max declared was a waste of good money.

Jacqui insisted that taking long showers was an indulgence and won the argument.

This was where she retreated after grueling days of tracking her prey, oftentimes foregoing the luxury of a plain shower when she was on the road.

Jacqui adjusted the knobs of the whirlpool and watched as the water churned gently against the edges of the tub. She lighted a few incense candles and poured lavender bath oil into the water.

She stepped gingerly into the warm water and slithered her whole body against the tub. She closed her eyes and sighed in bliss, basking in the floating sensation, making her feel weightless. She allowed her mind to roam, setting free all thoughts and stresses that accompanied her job.

But it was also during times like these that thoughts she had buried deep in the recesses of her psyche often crept out of their screened-off area where she had buried them.

Like Adam…

She hadn't seen or heard from him since that day she made her first successful bounty. The revelry that accompanied her return wasn't enough to cover up the intense disappointment she felt when she was told he left with Sarah. She cried herself to sleep that night, after admitting to herself the true status of her heart. She had fallen in love with him… fallen in love with a man who belonged to someone else.

Often, she cursed the day they met. Cursed the seduction he laid out for her. She blamed herself for trying to defeat him in his own game which ended with them having sex on the boxing ring floor. His intoxicating scent, the smell of his breath, the steely feel of his arms around her waist, the powerful thrusts as he entered her astride on his hips.

Jacqui crossed her arms around herself longing for Adam's lean arms. Then she uncrossed them to caress the skin of her throat, shoulders, and belly. They felt velvety and smooth to the touch. Unwittingly, her hands moved to her breasts as she lay immersed in the warm frothy water. She cupped both and let the thumbs and forefingers of each hand play with her nipples. She felt them harden under her ministrations as twinges of sexual pleasure traveled down her groin.

Jacqui enjoyed the feeling of her fingers as they slowly moved down to her cunt. Using two fingers, she opened the lips of her labia and let her clit pop out. The whirlpool massaged her clit gently. It felt really good.

She rubbed her exposed nub and added pressure with her finger. Her back arched as a spike of pleasure signaled her arousal.

Jacqui raised herself up from the tub and sat down against the rim. She opened her legs wide as she straddled two sides of the tub. She knew what she wanted, what she needed badly.

She picked up a bottle of lube and applied some on her fingers. Then she positioned her fingers against her vagina and rubbed her clit gently. The heat started to build within her open legs. As the heat mounted inside her, Jacqui added more and more pressure on her clit until it felt on fire. She knew her orgasm was near. She imagined Adam's lips as they flicked repeatedly on her clit when he had her prone on the mat. As the intense heat flaring between her legs became too much to bear, she gave in to a powerful orgasm, uttering Adam's name over and over again.

If you enjoyed this sample then look for **Rapid Pulse Bounty - Obsessed Bounty Hunter Romance Series, Book 3 by Carla Coxwell**.

Other Books by Darla Dunbar

- The Romeo Alpha BBW Paranormal Shifter Romance Series

- Romeo Alpha Blood Lines Romance Series

- The Alpha Feud BBW Paranormal Shifter Romance Series

- The Alpha Packed BBW Paranormal Shifter Romance Series

- The Daemon Paranormal Romance Chronicles

- The Mind Talker Paranormal Romance Series

Get the latest update on new releases from the author at:

https://darladunbar.com/newsletter/

About the Author - Darla Dunbar

Darla has been interested in paranormal romance since she was a teenager in high school. It was then that she discovered she could fulfill her fantasies through her writing.

Observing people and human behavior in the area of romance has always been one of her favorite pastimes. Combining that with an overactive imagination is a sure fire way of coming up with interesting themes.

Connect with Darla Dunbar

I really appreciate you reading my book! Here are my social media coordinates:

Friend me on Facebook:
https://www.facebook.com/darladunbar/

Follow me on Twitter: https://twitter.com/DarlDunbar

Check me out on Goodreads:
https://www.goodreads.com/author/show/8425857.Darla_Dunbar

Subscribe to my newsletter:
https://darladunbar.com/newsletter/

Visit my website: https://darladunbar.com/